THE Okay BOOK

Todd PARR

WALKER BOOKS
AND SUBSIDIARIES

LONDON · BOSTON · SYDNEY

It's okay to be Short

It's okay to wear Glasses

It's okay to Come From a Different place

It's okay to be TaLL

It's okay to wear
two different socks

It's okay to Eat all
the Icing OFF
Your birthday Cake

It's Okay
to wear
what
you
Like

It's okay to Share

CAT

DOG

It's okay to Laugh Out Loud

It's okay to cry

Boo Hoo

It's okay to Live in a Small House

It's Okay to have no Hair

It's okay to hang
out in the rain

It's okay to be skinny

It's okay to be BiG

It's Okay to be a different colour

It's okay to wear Braces

It's okay to put a
Fish in your Hair

It's okay to Dream BiG